Dear Parent:
Your child's love of reading starts here!

Every child learns to read in a different way and at his or her own speed. Some go back and forth between reading levels and read favorite books again and again. Others read through each level in order. You can help your young reader improve and become more confident by encouraging his or her own interests and abilities. From books your child reads with you to the first books he or she reads alone, there are I Can Read Books for every stage of reading:

SHARED READING
Basic language, word repetition, and whimsical illustrations, ideal for sharing with your emergent reader

BEGINNING READING
Short sentences, familiar words, and simple concepts for children eager to read on their own

READING WITH HELP
Engaging stories, longer sentences, and language play for developing readers

READING ALONE
Complex plots, challenging vocabulary, and high-interest topics for the independent reader

ADVANCED READING
Short paragraphs, chapters, and exciting themes for the perfect bridge to chapter books

I Can Read Books have introduced children to the joy of reading since 1957. Featuring award-winning authors and illustrators and a fabulous cast of beloved characters, I Can Read Books set the standard for beginning readers.

A lifetime of discovery begins with the magical words "I Can Read!"

Visit www.icanread.com for information on enriching your child's reading experience.

I Can Read!

READING 2 WITH HELP

Father and Son
Save the Day

HarperCollins®, ☰®, and I Can Read Book® are trademarks of HarperCollins Publishers.

Madagascar: Escape 2 Africa: Father and Son Save the Day
Madagascar: Escape 2 Africa™ & © 2008 DreamWorks Animation L.L.C.

Library of Congress catalog card number: 2008928093
ISBN 978-0-06-144780-8

Typography by Rick Farley

❖

First Edition

I Can Read!

READING 2 WITH HELP

DREAMWORKS

MADAGASCAR 2

ESCAPE 2 AFRICA

Father and Son Save the Day

Adapted by Gail Herman
Pencils by Charles Grosvenor
Paintings by Lydia Halverson

HarperCollins*Publishers*

On the way home from Madagascar,

Alex and his friends make

a surprise stop in Africa.

"Crash landing!" cries a penguin.

"We're stuck here!" cries Alex.

How will they get back to New York?

Will Alex ever sing and dance

at the zoo again?

Alex looks around.

Herds of zebras graze in the grass.

Giraffes stroll among the trees.

A pride of lions rests
by a water hole.
"I've been here before,"
Alex whispers to Marty.

Zuba, the lion leader, stomps over.

"This water hole is ours,"

Zuba says.

"Go back where you came from."

"Do I know you?" Alex asks.

"RRRRRRR!" Zuba roars.

But Zuba's wife, Florrie, sees a mark

on Alex's paw.

Zuba has the mark on his paw, too!

"Son?" asks Zuba.

"Dad!" says Alex.

When Alex was a baby,

he was stolen by hunters.

But now, he is back with his family.

"You've come home," Zuba says.

"My son is home!"

Happy tears roll down Alex's cheeks.

He hugs his parents tight.

"Someday, you will be the leader

of all the lions," says Zuba.

Alex strikes a pose.

"I've got the moves," he says.

"They call me King of New York."

One lion doesn't like Zuba or Alex,

but he pretends to be nice.

"Lions must show they are strong,"

Makunga tells Alex.

"You need to pass a test."

Alex doesn't understand.

He thinks the test is a talent show.

Hop, hop, shuffle, twist.

Alex shows his dance moves.

SLAM! A lion charges at him.

The test is over.

"Alex has failed!" says Makunga.

Now Zuba doesn't understand.

"You told me you are a king!" he says.

"My fans call me King," says Alex.

"I put on a show at the zoo.

I'm not a real king. I don't fight."

Now that Alex has failed,
he must leave the pride
in shame.

Alex's mom and dad go, too.

"Families stick together,"

says Florrie.

"Makunga is your leader now,"

Zuba tells the other lions.

Alex feels so bad.

"Dad doesn't think I'm a real lion,"

he says to himself.

"I've messed everything up.

How can I fix it?" he wonders.

Alex walks by the water hole.

He gasps. It is dry.

Then he sees the other animals.

They are confused and frightened.

"Listen up," says Makunga.

"If you want water,

you can go upriver to find out

what happened to it."

This is my chance,

thinks Alex.

Alex follows the dry riverbed.

At last, he reaches a wall of logs.

A dam! That's the problem.

That's why the water hole is dry.

All at once, people attack.

It's a safari group gone crazy!

"Bad kitty," says a mean old lady.

"Ahhh!" Alex steps into a trap.

He could be dinner!

"ROAR!" Zuba leaps into the clearing.

He slashes Alex's ropes

and frees him.

Then he holds Alex close.

"I've got you, son!"

But they are surrounded.

"Stay behind me," Zuba roars.

"We have to attack."

"No, Dad," says Alex.

He starts to dance.

Hop, hop, shuffle, twist.

"I know those moves," one man says.

"It's Alex the lion!"

"From the zoo," says another.

Everyone claps.

Alex and his dad are safe!

"That's my boy!" says Zuba.

Zuba sees that Alex is a king after all.

He is the king of New York!

But there's one more problem.

The dam!

Whirl, whirl. The plane is fixed!

The chimps scoop up Alex and Zuba.

They crash into the dam

and break it apart.

Water flows into the water hole.

"Hooray!" shout the animals.

"Hooray for Alex and Zuba!"

The king of the lions

and the king of New York

have saved the day!

Father and son did it together.